THE
VISITOR

A Horror Novella

SERGIO GOMEZ

Cover design: Teddi Black
Interior design: Megan McCullough

To all of the GraciePhila family—but
especially Joe, who taught me everything
I know about believing in myself

"Two possibilities exist: either we are alone in the Universe or we are not. Both are equally terrifying."

—Arthur C. Clarke

Sal's

"**C**an you believe this?" Sal said, putting the newspaper on the counter with a big grin. "Someone's been goin' around stealing Christmas lights off people's roofs."

The man sitting on the other side of the counter peeled his eyes away from the TV in the corner and glanced at the headline of the newspaper.

"People suck," Moshe Janovsky said, picking up his cup of soda and taking a sip, then turning back to watching the football game. The Cowboys were down 14.

"You got that right, buddy." Sal said, shaking his head.

In the kitchen, the fryer beeped. Sal went through the swinging metal doors and came back out with a basket of fried mushrooms.

"Kaito! Mushrooms are up," he called out, setting the basket on the bar counter.

Besides the thin man sitting at the counter, the only other patrons in the diner were Sal's Christmas regulars, a Japanese couple who came in to refuel after hiking the surrounding mountains.

"Looks like I'm my own waiter today," Kaito Takahashi said, coming up to the counter.

1

"You know how it is," Sal told him, laughing. "I give the girls the day off on Christmas. I'm a good boss like that."

"Yes, yes. Of course," Kaito said.

"Hey, tell me. Just how bad was it out there?" Sal leaned an elbow against the counter and looked out one of the windows at the snowstorm.

The buzz around town for the last week was that it was going to be the worst storm Indiana had seen in centuries— somewhere between six to eight inches of snow was expected. But they said that about all of them when the news cycle was slow, so Sal hadn't bought it. Not until now that he was watching the wind whip snowflakes the size of dimes around outside.

"Quite bad," was Kaito answered. "In fact, that's why we're here earlier than usual. We had to cut our hike short. There was too much ice on the trails. The higher we went, the worse it got."

"Damn."

"Yeah. Guess we didn't really earn these." Kaito grinned, glancing down at the mushrooms.

"Ahh, eat up, pal." Sal shrugged, standing up again. "It's the holidays, give yourself a present."

"Oh! Almost forgot," Kaito said. He reached into the breast pocket of his vest and pulled out a red envelope and a small package. "From me and Ichiko."

"Oh. You guys shouldn't have...but thanks," Sal said, a big smile forming on his face.

"You're welcome. Though, this was all her idea." Kaito laughed, pointing a thumb over his shoulder at his wife.

"Hey, Ichiko! Thank you so much."

The small woman looked up from doodling on a napkin and waved to him with a smile on her face. Kaito said merry Christmas to Sal, happy holidays to the other guy, and then picked his mushrooms up and returned to his wife.

Meanwhile, Sal took the present and card to a corner of the diner where a small, artificial Christmas tree was and put it alongside the other presents that sat underneath it. The presents were from his four waitresses who insisted on getting him stuff every year. Even though Sal made a big show of not wanting them to get him anything, he always smiled when he opened them up at the end of the night.

It was always just little things; t-shirts, belts, sweatshirts, occasionally a bottle of scotch, and so on, but they were the only presents Sal ever got, and they meant more to him than he'd ever let on. He had no children, had never been married, both his parents were long gone, and his siblings all lived on the West Coast.

Every now and again, one of his brothers might send him a fruitcake or some chocolate-covered pretzels (usually stale by the time they got to him), but it was the presents from the wait staff that captured the Christmas magic for him. Putting the present from the Takahashis on top of the little pile, he thought what a wonderful Christmas this was going to be.

Accident

Xavier was keeping the car under twenty miles an hour, driving with both hands wrapped tight around the steering wheel. As far as he could see, there weren't any other cars on the road, but it wasn't like there was any way for him to be sure of that. The snow wasn't just making the roads slippery, it was making visibility out here damn near impossible even with the wipers on the highest setting.

Which was why Xavier didn't see the sharp piece of metal in the middle of the highway until it was too late.

"*OH FUCK!*" Xavier hollered.

He tried to cut the wheel to the right, but he wasn't quick enough. The Maxima's right front tire popped as the metal pierced through it. The other tires to begin to slip on the icy roadway, and Xavier felt himself quickly losing control of the car.

In the backseat, his Border Collie barked in panic and clawed into the seat for dear life.

Xavier wrenched the wheel over as hard as he could, but the back end still began to swing away from him, sending the car into the left lane. Which meant if a car were coming up behind him on that lane, he'd just put them into danger. In a panic, he turned the wheel the other way, and suddenly he found himself in a spinout.

Round and round they went. Everything became a white blur through the windows as the car whipped around, making Xavier feel like he was trapped in some morbid snow globe. His dog gave up on barking and started to howl.

"Hold on!" he yelled at him, but Xavier knew the only thing that would stop this ride was a crash.

Or running off the side of the highway.

He closed his eyes, gritted his teeth, and hoped for the best.

Santiago Sanchez's haggard face stared back at him from the phone's screen while he waited for his wife to pick up his FaceTime call. His five o'clock shadow had turned into a full beard, and dark circles were beginning to form underneath his eyes. This was usually how he looked at the end of his delivery routes, but something about seeing himself like this on Christmas made it worse.

He'd been trying to race back from Arkansas to Ohio in hopes of at least spending the last few hours of Christmas with his family. But the East coast had been getting hit with some heavy snowfall this year, and as luck would have it, he got caught in the middle of a blizzard in Indiana. According to all of the local stations on the radio he'd been listening to since entering the state, today was going to be the worst snowstorm Indiana had seen in years.

The roads were a testament to this, too, as Santiago's semitruck had begun to slip and slide all over the place within hours of the storm starting, forcing him to pull over to the side of the highway and kiss any hopes of seeing his family tonight goodbye.

On the screen, the words "FACETIME UNAVAILABLE" popped up, letting him know that his wife hadn't answered his call. It was 4PM, which meant Silvia was likely preparing dinner. She was probably focused on slicing up lettuce and radishes for the pozole and hadn't heard the phone ringing over the Selena music playing in the kitchen.

His heart felt heavy as he locked the phone screen and put it on the dashboard. He'd Facetimed with them this morning and Silvia had held the phone up so he could see his daughters opening their presents, but he was hoping to see them again before bed.

Oh, well. She'll probably call me back when they're done with dinner.

The thought of dinner made his stomach grumble, reminding him he hadn't eaten anything all day except the bagel he got from the rest stop where he'd stopped this morning.

Santiago looked out the passenger side window, where a short distance away he could just see what appeared to be a roadside diner lit up against the storm. The white haze of the snowfall made it difficult to know for sure but being a truck driver, he was experienced enough to know that neon lights on a shiny building were the trademark tells of a highway eatery.

Santiago glanced at his phone one more time to see if maybe his wife was calling him back after all, but no such luck. So instead he slipped the iPhone into the pocket of the jacket sitting on the passenger seat, then put the jacket on.

He doubted the diner would have pozole on their menu, or much of a Christmas spread, and in fact he'd probably be lucky if they had anything that didn't come out of a can, but at least he'd be able to get something warm to fill his stomach in there.

The lot in front of the place looked too small for his truck, especially with two cars already occupying it. It wasn't much of a walk, but something told him the snow would make it feel longer than it looked.

Santiago opened the truck door and was met with a frigid blast of cold that sent a cluster of snowflakes into his face. Santiago wiped them off with his sleeve and hopped out of the truck. He sunk into five inches of snow and realized just how bad the storm was.

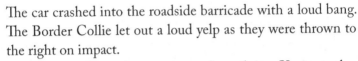

The car crashed into the roadside barricade with a loud bang. The Border Collie let out a loud yelp as they were thrown to the right on impact.

For a moment, there was complete silence. Xavier took a moment to catch his breath, and make sure he was still alive, and then he undid his seatbelt and twisted around to his dog. "Hey, Norm, you okay back there?"

The dog was apparently over his shock from just moments ago. Staring out the window, he growled at the falling snow. He was still strapped into his bright yellow dog seat. That expensive contraption had been a point of argument between him and his girlfriend when she first bought it but seeing that it'd kept Norman from flying out of the car, he was glad he'd lost that argument.

Xavier reached out to pet the dog's head. Norm let out a short *whoof* to let him know he was fine.

"Okay, good." Patting him on the head one last time, he went back to taking stock of how bad things were.

They'd struck the barricade almost head on, but not quite. Everything from the right headlight to the passenger side door had been crumpled up or torn open, and along with the popped tire, that meant the car was likely toast.

Xavier put the car in reverse anyway and gave it some gas. It rocked backward, and as it did there was a loud and teeth-jarring squeal of metal scraping on metal. He let it settle forward, and tried again, and the sound got worse. When he stopped this time, the car sank further into the snow.

"Looks like we're in a jam, buddy," Xavier told the Border Collie, putting the car in park out of habit. It's not like it was going anywhere.

Norm let out a short bark in agreement.

Xavier zipped his jacket up and climbed out of the car. He sank up to his shins and had to heave on the back-passenger door before it opened up wide enough against the snowbank for him to reach inside and undo Norman's seatbelt. After looking him over for any injuries and seeing none, he let the dog out of the car. The dog didn't do much better than he had, bounding up out of the snow just to fall into it again.

While Xavier grabbed the leash from the trunk, Norman got himself up to the roadway where the snow was only a few inches deep and he could shake himself off.

With the leash in place he walked them around to where they could see the damage and found the front of the car was crumpled up like an accordion. The side of it was laid open like a giant can opener had torn through it. The tire was hanging onto the wheel in shreds.

Damn. Maybe I should've told Dad I wasn't gonna make it this year, he thought, shaking his head.

Oh well, it was too late for that. He was here now, in the middle of nowhere, in a raging snowstorm, with no car, and had to deal with this mess.

He looked around, and realized he'd been lucky the barricade was there. Past it was a ten foot drop off the side of the highway. That was where he would have gone if the reinforced steel barrier hadn't caught him.

There was nothing he could see past a dozen feet or so. No cars. No buildings. No lights anywhere. Then he stopped, and looked again, and if he squinted against the blizzard, he could just make out a semi parked on the shoulder of the road up ahead. Yet another thing to be thankful for...he'd lost control back here, and not up there where he would have crashed his Maxima into the rear end of that vehicle.

Xavier took his cell phone out of his pocket and dialed Triple A's number. On the third ring, he got an automated message telling him that due to inclement weather, services were suspended, and to call 9-1-1 if there was an emergency.

Yeah, sure, Xavier laughed. Something told him 9-1-1 wouldn't be coming out for a popped tire.

Next, he tried calling his girlfriend, Shawna, but the call didn't go through. Now the phone told him there was no service.

That's weird. It must've had something to do with where he was standing. Or maybe the storm. He made a mental note to try to call her again in a little bit, after he got somewhere safe. Putting the phone away he tugged on Norm's leash and they started down the side of the road.

Xavier stopped when he saw a burly man coming up the highway toward him. The man was wearing a heavy coat with his hood up and his hands in his pockets.

"Hey, there. Need some help?" the man asked, taking one hand out to give him a friendly wave.

Beside Xavier, Norman started to growl.

"Easy boy," Xavier said to his dog. Then he raised his voice over the wind to answer the guy. "Uh, hey there. I think we're okay, thanks."

"Whoa, there. I come in peace," the man said, sticking two fingers up into the air. "I promise. I was just getting out of my truck and saw you on the side of the road. You sure you're okay?"

Feeling a little sheepish for being scared, Xavier huddled into his coat with a shrug. "Yeah, we're good. My car is pretty banged up, but we're good."

"Name's Santiago," the man said, coming up to him with his hand held out.

Xavier accepted the handshake and introduced himself.

"What happened?" Santiago asked.

"Hit that thing," Xavier said, pointing a few feet behind them, where the piece of scrap metal with the sharp edge was poking out of the snow in the highway like a javelin. Now that he could see it more clearly it looked like a leftover piece from another car accident.

"You have a spare tire?" Santiago asked him.

"Yeah, but it won't do me any good. The car's a mess."

They'd walked back to where they could see the damage, and Santiago let out a low whistle as he nodded in understanding.

"I just tried Triple A," Xavier explained. "Got a recording saying they aren't coming out because of the storm."

As if it heard him, the storm kicked up. The wind howled, and slapped snow into both men's faces.

Santiago pointed a thumb over his shoulder, "I was heading to a diner I saw just up the road. You can't see it from here in all this, but trust me, it's there. I don't know if anyone can help you in there, but it'd beat sitting in your car out here in the cold or trying to find the nearest town."

That sounded like a good idea to Xavier. He could wait in there until the storm eased up or the plows got brave enough to come out again. Besides, he could go for a hot cup of coffee.

"Yeah, that sounds great, actually," he said. Then, he held the leash up as if Santiago could've missed the dog somehow. "I just hope they're pet-friendly in there."

Santiago waved the concern off. "I'm sure they'll be okay with it. It's the jolliest time of the year, and all that."

They both snickered at this as they walked through the snow to the diner, with Norman trotting alongside them. He'd been growling most of the interaction but was easing up on it now that he saw Xavier trusted the man.

Jolly

Xavier pushed the diner door open. On the other side of it, a Christmas wreath jingled, which got the attention of the few people inside. They all stopped what they were doing and turned to look at the newcomers.

For a stretch of a few seconds, no one moved a muscle. They all just stared at each other. *A Holly Jolly Christmas* by Burl Ives was playing from a plugged-in plastic radio behind the counter, but the tune did nothing to ease the tension in the room.

Behind Santiago and Xavier, there was a metallic thud as the front door closed on its hinges.

"Uh, good evening everyone," Santiago said, lifting a hand up to greet them. Then, because he felt like they'd just stumbled into a secret meeting or something he asked, "Are we okay to come in?"

"Yeah, yeah," Sal said, waving them in. "Pardon the manners, it's just that we weren't exactly expecting any more people to join us."

"The dog okay?" Xavier asked, holding up the leash.

"Yeah, he's fine."

Xavier and Santiago walked down the narrow diner in single file, with Norm between them. Each one of their steps shook off snow from their boots and paws and left little trails of water on the checkered floor.

The diner was a narrow trailer that had been repurposed into a roadside eatery. On one side was a bar area lined with bright red pleather stools. Behind the counter was a shelf almost as long as the wall lined with bottles of hot sauce, tubs of condiments, jars of pickles, Indianapolis Colts memorabilia and Styrofoam to-go containers.

The other side of the trailer was occupied by booths with the same color pleather seats and tables with chrome napkins and sidings. Decorating the walls were clusters of vintage seventies advertisements from companies like Coca-Cola, Chiclets, and Bazooka. Rounding out the old school, chic look of the place was a bubblegum machine that looked like it'd never been used or dusted. Stuffed into the corner next to it was a small Christmas tree that stuck out as it was the only modern decoration in the whole place.

Sal met the newcomers at the front of the counter and knelt down to pet the Border Collie. Norm panted happily with the attention.

"What a beautiful dog. What's his name?"

"Norm," Xavier said, settling into one of the stools underneath the Christmas lights.

Sal gave the scruff underneath the dog's chin a good scrubbing, then got up and went to a small sink behind the counter to wash his hands. After drying his hands on the apron hanging in front of his lap he grabbed two menus from a cubby underneath the bar and placed them in front of the new patrons.

"Can I get you guys started with something to drink? Coffees or something?"

They both asked for a coffee and water, and Sal headed over to get it ready for them.

Turning away from the football game because it was boring him, Moshe asked them, "So, what drags you guys into this place?"

"Car troubles." Santiago said, looking at Xavier to see if that answer sufficed.

Xavier shrugged. "Yeah, that about covers it."

"Ah, the snow fucked you guys over just like me, then." Moshe said, nodding.

"Yeah, my car spun out on the highway," Xavier sighed. "Ended up crashing into the barricade and messing her up pretty bad."

"Yup," Santiago nodded. "And my rig just couldn't handle the slippery roads."

"You guys were driving together or something?" Moshe asked, looking the two guys over. He was going to be surprised if they said yes, because these two seemed to be from very different walks of life judging by their clothes and the way they carried themselves.

"Nope, we just met," Santiago answered. "Guess you could say disaster brought us together."

"Well, shit!" Moshe said with a laugh. "It really is the jolliest time of the year."

"What about you? What's your story?" Santiago asked him.

"I was in Indiana for a book signing earlier in the week."

"Signing?" Xavier asked. "You a write a book or something?" He looked closer at the guy sitting two seats from him now to see if he recognized him from somewhere.

"Or something," Moshe said, grinning. He picked up his cup of soda and took a long drink from it for dramatic effect. "I'm a poet."

"Ah, so you must be some romantic kind of guy, then?" Santiago ribbed.

Moshe laughed. "No, no. I don't write *that* kind of poetry."

"Then what do you write, exactly?"

"I write about things like the woes of backsplash when you're taking a big dump. Or having to meet my girlfriend's bitchy mom. Depends on my mood, really."

Sal came back, balancing a round tray in his hand. He set it down and put the coffee and waters in front of Santiago and Xavier. Then he leaned an elbow on the counter and regarded the writer with the same look the other two were giving him.

"So, uh, you write comedy then?"

"Yeah, I'm a comedian and a poet, which means I'm twice as likely to fuck up my profession."

The others laughed at that, although they didn't quite get the joke.

"So, I guess we're the misfits spending this fine holiday together." Moshe said, taking a quick sip of his Coke. "Lucky me, I don't celebrate Christmas. How about you fine fellas?"

"I've got a wife and two daughters back home celebrating without me," Santiago said, trying to hide the ache of the words.

"My pops and stepmom were expecting me and Norm tonight." Xavier shrugged, and looked out the window to see that the storm hadn't relented even a little bit. "Guess I should've just went to my girlfriend's house, huh? Maybe I could've read one of your poems to her parents?"

Moshe laughed. "Yes! It would've put you all in a merry mood—depending on which one you picked."

"Speak for yourself," Sal said, bringing the conversation back to the holiday. "For me and that fine couple over there, this is tradition."

Sal was referring to the Takahashis, who were still sitting in their booth, engaged in their own conversation in Japanese.

"What? Really?" Moshe said, incredulous. "Who would make coming here their tradition on purpose…uh, shit, no offense, pal."

"None taken," Sal said, chortling. "My friends over there have a cabin not too far away. They hike the mountains then come down here to pay their old friend, Sal, a visit and eat some of my fried mushrooms."

"God," Santiago said, feeling his stomach rumble at the mention of food. "I don't even like mushrooms, but I could probably eat an entire plate of those right about now. What's good around here?"

"The tuna sandwich I had was bitchin'," Moshe offered.

"I'll have a double cheeseburger with an order of fries," Xavier said. He'd been scanning the menu while they'd been talking. "Can't go wrong with the classics."

"I'll have the same." Santiago said.

"How do you guys want them?"

"Medium," Xavier told him.

"Well done for me," Santiago requested.

"Great," Sal said, grabbing the menus from them and starting into the kitchen. "I'll be back in a jiffy."

Moshe snorted. "Whatever. I'm used to no one listening to me."

The diner filled with laughter as they all got the self-deprecating humor this time.

Meanwhile, outside, the storm continued to rage.

Howling

Every now and again, they could hear the fierce winds howling outside over the Christmas music playing inside the diner. It was whipping snow onto the windows with such force that the snowflakes turned to bits of water on impact. Rivulets dripped down the length of the glass before freezing solid. A crust of ice built up, thick and heavy, making an opaque screen that was nearly impossible to see through.

Independently of each other, everyone in Sal's Diner realized they weren't going anywhere for a very long time. With nothing else to do, they started making small talk about themselves.

Moshe told them about how he'd done his first book signing on acid. Santiago showed everyone pictures of his wife and kids. Xavier told them about engineering school and about how he had an internship lined up for the spring semester at some power company. Kaito and Ichiko told them about their cabin, about their annual hike through the surrounding mountains, and how they were going to Japan next month—which would be the first time Kaito returned there in nearly five years.

As they talked about ordinary, mundane things, they began to feel at ease with each other. The word "friend" was perhaps too strong to use to describe their developing relationships, but with each passing minute, they became less and less of strangers to one another. They began to think that maybe this wasn't such a bad situation to be in after all.

But there was still one more visitor yet to come to Sal's Diner.

A few yards down the road from Sal's Diner, a loud *snap* filled the air as a hefty branch was blown clear off an oak tree. The branch collapsed onto a power pole below the tree, and its smaller branches got caught on the lines, grabbing on like a clawed hand. And as the branch continued its fall, it yanked the power pole right out of the ground, bringing it down with it. Sparks and electricity shot through the air like some hazardous lightshow reflecting off crystals of frozen moisture all around.

Inside Sal's Diner, the lights went out.

Flickers

The football game winked off the television, the radio fell silent in the middle of Florence + the Machine's cover of *Last Christmas*, the overhead lights flickered a few times before going out. For a second, the only lights on in the whole place were the Christmas lights hanging over the stools, like a Christmas miracle. Then, those too went out, leaving the diner in total darkness.

"Oh fuck!" Moshe exclaimed.

Norman got up to his feet, the piece of hamburger Sal had graciously cooked up for him forgotten, and started growling from his chest.

"Stay calm boy," Xavier said, finding the dog's collar and holding onto it to keep him from doing anything sudden. With his other hand, he stroked him on the head. The gesture seemed to calm him some.

The kitchen doors pushed open and a pale beam of light cut through the diner, right between Santiago and Moshe as Sal emerged from the back carrying a flashlight.

"Holy smokes!" Sal said, swinging the flashlight around to inspect the place. Behind the glow of the light, his face looked ghoulish, like a man about to tell a ghost story over a campfire, but the others were glad for the bit of light.

"Y-you have a backup generator, right?" Kaito asked.

Just as the words escaped his lips, the group felt the vibrating hum of a generator turning on in the cellar underneath them. Collectively, the group breathed a sigh of relief as the lights came back on. Only every other fixture came back to life, but it was better than nothing.

"Okay, good," Moshe said, shifting in his seat. "Next question. That'll keep the heat on, right?"

"Sort of," Sal responded. He clicked the flashlight off and set it down on a shelf behind him.

"What do you mean sort of?"

"Well, I have to switch the backup generator to power both the electrical and heating system."

"What kind of janky ass system is that?" Moshe snickered.

Sal shrugged as he walked over to a door at the far side of the diner. "We make do with what we have out here in the sticks, bud."

"Want one of us to come with you?" Xavier offered.

With his hand resting on the doorknob, Sal turned to him and shook his head.

"Fine by me," Moshe said. "If you do need help, make sure you scream loud enough for us to hear you up here."

"You really are quite the comedian, ain't ya?" Sal snorted. Then he pulled the door open. The door hinges squeaked, as if protesting something none of them knew about.

Cellar

atching Sal disappear down the wooden set of stairs into the darkened cellar made Santiago anxious for some reason he couldn't explain. A cold knot started to form in the pit of his stomach. He picked his mug up, thinking the warm coffee would help, only to find it was empty.

"Need a refill?" Moshe asked, grinning at him. The grin, like Sal's laugh before going down the stairs, didn't have much humor in it.

Santiago didn't respond to him. He just got up and walked around the counter to where the coffeepot was, feeling like everyone in the diner was watching him. He poured coffee into his mug, then put the pot back under the machine. At the same time, almost as if that were what caused it, the lights in the diner went out again.

Norman turned in a circle, his tail between his legs, whining in the darkness.

Then, from below them they heard Sal scream.

When the lights came back on, everyone was on their feet.

The radio powered back on with *Jingle All the Way* playing on it.

Moshe was at the front door, frozen there like a child who'd just been caught drawing on the walls of his parents' bedroom.

"Well, it was nice meeting you guys," he said, pulling the front door open. "See ya!"

The open door invited a frigid blast from the outside into the diner before it closed behind the fleeing poet.

"Coward," Ichiko muttered after him, deliberately using the English word to make sure the others understood her. They did, but on multiple levels. Because they were all as frightened as Moshe—they were just handling it differently.

"We don't need him," Santiago said. He was pressed up against the wall, just like his older brother had always taught him to do when the lights would go out in the crummy apartments they grew up in. *So no one can sneak up on you, got it?* His brother's words echoed in his head, and for the first time Santiago saw how important a survival tactic it was.

"Everyone hold on, please," Kaito said, going over to where the cellar door was.

He stopped at the top of the staircase, but the cellar was much too dark for him to see anything. Either Sal hadn't gotten a chance to turn on the lights down there, or someone else had turned them off...

"H-Hello?" Kaito called down.

No response.

The worst possible outcome.

Even a scream would have been preferable because at least then they would know there was still a chance Sal was alive down there.

Santiago reached over and shut the radio off in the middle of *Jingle All the Way*. Somehow, the sudden silence made the diner feel smaller, like the walls were closing in on each other. Santiago walked over and stood by Kaito's side.

"Sal!" he shouted down. "Sal! You okay?"

The only sound was a low metallic clang. It was so quiet that only Santiago and Kaito heard it, and even they weren't sure if they'd just imagined it or not.

Kaito took a step back. "This is not good."

Santiago shook his head, but he meant it as agreement.

"We should go check on him." Xavier suggested. "You know, just to make sure. He's probably okay, but just to be safe, you know?"

Kaito and Santiago glanced at one another, searching the other's face to see if they were thinking the same thing. They were.

"Yeah," Santiago said. "Let's do that."

Xavier grabbed a knife sitting behind the counter. It was a small paring knife Sal used to cut the lemons into wedges for drinks, but at least it was something.

Kaito shook his head and pointed to the metal doors behind him. "You'll find bigger knives in there."

"What about you?" Xavier asked, putting the knife back.

Kaito lifted his vest up, revealing a large hunting knife strapped to his belt. "I have mine."

"Yeah. Guess you do."

"You never know what trouble you'll run into up on the mountains," Kaito told him. "Anyway. Go and grab knives. I'll wait here."

Without another word, Xavier and Santiago pushed through the metal doors leading into the kitchen. Not wanting to be left alone, Norm followed.

Ichiko got up from the booth, looking for the cordless phone she'd seen Sal using before. She found it sitting on top of a roll of paper towels on one of the shelves and picked it up.

She pressed it to her ear, hitting the call button, and waited for the dial tone. Instead, she heard something else.

Something like static…but not quite. There was something like whispers in the white noise. It sounded like someone speaking. Like a message, except in a language she couldn't understand.

She moved the phone away, pressed the "CALL" button again, and waited.

This time, she heard it more clearly.

"*T'rakol… Fur'klow…*"

The words—she was sure they were words of some kind—came through clearer than before now.

She hit the "END" button and put the phone down and looked at her husband. "Kaito…?"

He had been keeping his eyes on the kitchen doors, waiting for the other two to come back with their knives, but he looked over at his wife now. Ichiko's skin was as white as the snow outside.

"Ichiko? What's wrong?" he asked, stepping closer to her.

"Kaito. The phone line…is dead." Ichiko said, not sure how to tell her husband about the voice.

But she knew one thing for certain, what she'd heard was some sort of message.

Heroes

He didn't remember parking as far away as he had, but the snow and bitter-cold had a way of making things seem more distant than they were. The snowstorm was even worse now that he was face-to-face with it.

"Holy cow, Moshe," he said to himself, sticking his hands into the pocket of his jacket for warmth. "You really chose a bitter pill to swallow."

There was the comedian emerging again, trying to drown out the shitty situation he'd created for himself. But there was no way he was going to turn back to the diner, so he started across the parking lot.

The others probably thought he was a coward for leaving, but he didn't care. They could go play heroes if they wanted to, but Moshe had no interest in that. Shit, he wouldn't have even been in the damn state if it weren't for some unfortunate missteps.

He was only halfway across the lot but he was already planning out what he was going to do. If the car couldn't plow through the snow (it wouldn't be able to, he was sure of that) he would just sit inside it and listen to the radio with the heater turned on. He had a full tank of gas, he figured that should last him long enough until the knuckleheads in charge of clearing the snow from the highway decided to show up.

Once the roads were clear, he'd try to find the airport and get the fuck out of this state.

There was also the possibility that someone from the diner would come find him to tell him that everything was OK. That Sal had just screamed because he'd tripped in the dark and bumped his knee or something.

A pang of guilt made him stop and glance over his shoulder. He considered going back, then squashed that thought.

No way. They'd probably throw my ass out, anyhow.

He thought, turning away from the diner, and walking faster to his car now.

They were all gathered in the doorway, peering down the dark staircase that led into the even darker cellar. Each of them was equipped with a knife and flashlights they'd also found in one of the drawers in the kitchen, but having gotten this far, none of them were sure how to proceed.

"So, who wants to go first?" Santiago said.

The stairwell was narrow, which meant they'd have to go down one person at a time. The first person would of course be in the most danger because if the group had to turn and run, they'd suddenly find themselves at the back of the line—or worse, if the group *didn't* run, the staircase would be blocked off to them. Volunteering oneself to go first would be a feat of guts rather than brains.

"I'll go," Xavier volunteered.

As if understanding the words—and maybe on some level he did—Norman let out a yelp of disapproval from the table where Xavier had tied him up. He didn't want his faithful friend following them down into the cellar. He was already trying to break free from his leash to go to Xavier's side.

"Don't worry, boy," Xavier told him. "I'll be okay… I promise."

Then, without any more hesitation, he clutched the knife in his hand, clicked his flashlight on, and started down the staircase.

Sideways

Moshe had the seat reclined all the way back, the radio playing smooth jazz, and the heat turned up to the highest setting, but his mind kept racing with thoughts of the predicament he was in.

More than he ever thought he would, he missed his tiny apartment in LA. He'd even take a roach-infested motel over being stuck out here in the middle of nowhere, Indiana with nothing but snow everywhere he looked.

He turned to his side, closed his eyes, and tried to shut his mind off again. After a few seconds of not being able to relax, he sat back up when an idea sprung to mind.

He turned the radio dial and searched for the local sports station. Moshe didn't really care about sports, but he'd be lying if he said he hadn't been a little bit invested in the game he'd been watching back at the diner. And if he couldn't sleep, at least he could keep his mind occupied with the commentator's play-by-play. After a few turns, he found the station just as the broadcaster was announcing the score. The Packers were up 21-3 on the Cowboys now.

Moshe reclined back into the seat, and closed his eyes.

The end of Xavier's flashlight beam shone on a thin chain dangling from the ceiling. He pulled on it, and a bare bulb hanging from the basement ceiling turned on. Its light was pale and dim and failed to reach the corners of the room, leaving them in shadows, but it was better than nothing.

Xavier clicked his flashlight off.

"Look," Santiago said, coming up next to him. He was pointing to another staircase opposite the one they'd just climbed down.

The light from the bulb was just lighting the first two steps, but even that was enough for them to see they were slick with blood.

Sal's blood. No doubt.

Santiago pointed his flashlight up the staircase, following the trail of blood with the beam. The steps ended at a doorway that was angled toward them, almost parallel with the ceiling, which suggested the doorway was built into the ground outside. Storm doors. They separated the outside from the cellar, but they hadn't been shut all the way. Cold air slithered through like a ghost.

At some point they'd been opened, and Sal dragged through them.

"We should get out of here," Santiago said.

Before any of them could agree or argue, the door leading into the diner shut closed behind them.

"What the hell?" Xavier said under his breath.

Upstairs, Norman started to bark incessantly. They heard his paws scratching at the floor and the creaking of the floorboards as someone walked toward him.

Xavier shouldered past Kaito and Santiago, meaning to go up the steps, but stopped when he saw the door was indeed shut closed. Something about seeing it with his own eyes made it worse.

"Moshe, are you fucking with us?" Santiago called up, hoping the poet would open the door with a shit-eating grin on his face.

There was no response, only more walking, followed by the front door of the diner being opened. And then, Norm's barks were gone.

"It's Moshe." Santiago said, turning around to look at the others. "It has to be him, right? He's screwing with us."

Before any of the others could respond, the wind forced the two outside doors open. They banged against the concrete doorway with a loud thud that echoed through the cellar.

Xavier, worried about his dog, started to move, but Kaito grabbed him by the shoulder and pulled him back.

It was Santiago who went charging up the stairs, taking them two at a time. He couldn't die down here. He needed to see his family before the Christmas magic turned into the New Year craze.

At the top of the steps, Santiago turned the doorknob and threw the door open. On the other side, someone was standing there

The football game had done the trick, and Moshe had been able to nod off long enough that he began to drool. But the sound of snow being moved somewhere outside the car stirred him awake now. He sat up in the seat, wiping the spittle off the side of his mouth and looking at the pool that had formed on the headrest with mild disgust.

Oh, well. It was a rental.

The sound that had woken him up came again, and now that he was fully alert, there was no mistaking it. It was the shushing sound of snow being moved, and it sounded like it was close to the car.

Snowplows, he thought hopefully. *About damn time.*

Moshe turned to the window, but there was about an inch of snow and ice caked to it and he couldn't see anything, so he rolled it down and punched the wall of wintery white that had formed like a second skin. Some of it fell onto his lap, melting and wetting the front of his jeans. He didn't care, though, because his mind was focused elsewhere right now.

Moshe stuck his head out and scanned the street. There wasn't a single sign of plow trucks out there. No tire marks, no plowed areas, nothing. The heavy snowfall made it difficult to see, but he should've at least been able to see lights if there were any snow removal vehicles out there.

The sound of snow moving came again. Now that he was wide awake, he was able to pinpoint where it was coming from. It was behind the car. He heard it better, too. It didn't sound like snow being plowed at all. More like someone was walking through the snow.

Someone from the diner?

He stuck his head out through the hole he'd made and saw a four-legged shadow outlined against the snow. The shadow expanded out from the back bumper, meaning whatever was making it was standing behind the car.

Xavier's dog, Moshe thought, wetting his lips to whistle him over. *What the hell is that mutt doing out here?*

The shadow started to move. The creature followed, one limb at a time.

It wasn't a Border Collie.

The creature standing next to the car was outlined in the red glow of the car's taillights. It had the eyes of a fish and rough, dark green skin. Like an alligator's, maybe. The shape of its body was that of a large feline, with knob-like protrusions here and there.

Moshe could hardly process what the thing was. The only word that sprung to his mind was *abomination*.

The creature's head began to open, starting from the crest of its forehead and going all the way down the chin, as if someone was unzipping its skull. The gap opened wider and deeper, and teeth that reflected red sprang into view in a mouth that opened sideways.

Moshe felt the metallic taste of fear coat his mouth.

Then, the creature sprang at him, its massive paws tearing through the snow with ease.

Moshe tried to duck back into the car, but there wasn't enough time. Claws on the tips of the creature's paws sank into his shoulders and held him in place, and then its sideways mouth clamped around his head down to his neck.

Moshe screamed. No one heard.

With a quick jerk, the creature yanked Moshe out of the car. His head came away from his shoulders as it did, leaving long stringers of bloody flesh attaching his severed body.

Blood colored the snow as Moshe's corpse hit the ground.

Bleeding

Santiago stared up at a wooden ceiling that had countless spiderwebs woven in between its beams. The bare bulb hanging in the center of the room swung left and right, from the vibrations on the floor above, throwing its pale light against the walls.

The bulb's swaying was gentle, like a slow dance.

Santiago watched the bulb, almost hypnotized, wondering if death was this peaceful for everyone, or if he just happened to be one of the lucky ones.

Lucky to be dying. No seas tonto. He would've smiled at the ridiculousness of the thought, of the absurdity of it, but he couldn't. He was losing all the strength in his body, and only grew weaker with each passing second.

The bulb's dance would be over soon. At least, for him it would.

A feminine face appeared in his vision. It was vaguely familiar, a face he'd only just met.

"Stay with us," she said. "You're going to be okay."

But she was lying.

37

He let out a small cough and felt something thick come up out of his mouth and spill out. It was warm and tasted funny.

Blood. It was blood he was tasting.

I'm bleeding to death.

His hand moved, almost involuntarily, toward the woman's face. His fingers brushed against her cheek and left thin streaks of blood on her face. Touching her awoke some part of Santiago's mind, and it all came back to him.

The woman at his side was Ichiko Takahashi, he was in the cellar of Sal's Roadside Diner, dying in Indiana. Dying on Christmas.

And that pain in his neck… it was a knife. The person at the top of the stairs had driven a knife into his neck before he'd gone tumbling down the staircase.

Santiago wanted to tell her he was dying, that he wasn't okay, but he had no more energy left in him. Looking into her eyes, something told him Ichiko knew anyway.

Santiago closed his eyes and waited for death, wishing he could have said goodnight to his daughters one last time.

Wounded

Kaito was on the opposite side of the basement from the others, rummaging through a stack of boxes, trying to find a piece of cloth to press against Santiago's wound. He knew it was pointless, but it wouldn't have sat right with him if he didn't at least try. So far, he'd had no luck. There seemed to be nothing but straws and plastic silverware in these boxes.

He was about to move the box he was going through to look inside the one underneath, when a thump coming from the staircase below the storm doors made him stop.

Behind him, he could still hear the murmurs of Xavier and Ichiko trying to keep Santiago alive.

Something was moving on the staircase. Whatever it was, it had dropped down through the doors quick enough to hide in the shadows, and now it was sitting there, waiting.

Kaito unclipped the hunting knife from his belt and took the flashlight out of his back pocket at the same time. He clicked the flashlight on and shone the beam up the stairs, one at a time.

Sitting in the middle, crouched over like a prowling lioness, was some sort of four-legged animal. An alligator popped into

Kaito's mind because of the thick and scaly skin, but that wasn't right. The limbs were too long, its body too slender.

This was something else. Something that was alien—yet familiar at the same time.

The creature hadn't reacted to the light because its eyes were locked in on its target.

Kaito turned to see what it was eyeing up, and a lump of fear formed in his throat as he realized its target was Ichiko. Instinct took over, and Kaito kicked the boxes in front of him in an attempt to divert the creature's attention to himself—but it didn't work.

The creature snarled at him, and then jumped down the staircase, clearing all the remaining steps in a single leap.

Then it charged at Ichiko with its sideways mouth opening down its face.

Still crouched over Santiago's body, Ichiko turned around at the sound of the creature sprinting toward her. She jumped up to her feet to try to get away, but the creature was quicker. It cleared the space between them and was on her, clamping its mouth around her shoulder.

Ichiko screamed, as the teeth sunk into her flesh and the animal pulled her toward the ground. The knife was still in her other hand, and she thrust it in the general direction of where the thing was. It was a wild attack, but through sheer luck it pierced through one of the creature's bulbous eyes. The creature's bite loosened up, and Ichiko shook herself free. Still on the ground, she kicked her legs to skitter away from the creature.

Kaito was already running toward her, and now he jumped onto the creature's back. He wrapped one arm around the thing's throat and used his forearm to pry the creature's head up. With his other arm, he stabbed his knife into the creature's throat.

There was a resistance, like the thing's skin was made of leather, but Kaito pushed harder until he felt the tip of the knife pierce through and the blade sank into soft flesh.

The creature reared up, jerking its body left and right until it flung Kaito off its back. He hit the ground hard and rolled until his back collided with the wall.

Xavier had been just standing there, watching, frozen by the impossibility of what he was seeing. But Ichiko screaming out for her husband shook him out of the shock, and Xavier sprang into action.

He charged at the creature with the point of his knife thrust out. The creature, wounded but still on its feet, saw him coming and backed away. It let out a hiss like a barking snake. The thing was bleeding, with a knife sticking out of its eye, and outnumbered.

"Fuck off!" Xavier shouted at it, hoping to intimidate the thing into running away.

But the creature stood its ground. It arched its back up like a cat and hissed louder than before Xavier took a half step back, but kept the knife pointed at the thing.

While they were caught in this standoff, Kaito slowly woke from unconsciousness. He roused himself, taking a moment to see where the creature was now and to recover his hunting knife where the creature had shaken it away. He found it a few feet in front of him, picked it up and ran toward the creature.

The creature turned on him, snapping its teeth in the air. Kaito lunged at it knife first. He ducked a swipe from the creature's claws and drove his long blade into the inside of the thing's mouth as hard as he could, feeling its hot breath all the way up to his elbow.

The knife tip punctured the back of the creature's throat before it could bite down on his arm, and a spray of dark blood arced up and across the room.

Wounded again, bleeding badly, the creature decided to retreat. It backed away so fast that Kaito lost his grip on the knife. The creature found itself in a corner, shaking its head violently as it tried to dislodge the knife from its throat. It mewled, and snarled, gargling its own blood as it choked on it.

Kaito and Xavier were standing shoulder to shoulder now, with Xavier brandishing his knife in front of him, ready to use it if the creature rushed them.

A scream from behind them surprised them both and then Ichiko was barreling between them, carrying a two-by-four over her head. As she closed in on the creature, she brought the piece of wood down on the top of its skull like a sledgehammer.

A loud *thwack* reverberated through the cellar as the creature's skull collapsed under the weight of the assault and it dropped down to the ground, dead.

But Ichiko didn't relent. She slammed the piece of wood down on the creature's head again. And again. And again. With each strike letting out a scream—no, a battle cry—at the top of her lungs.

The wound in her shoulder opened wider with every motion, but she fought through the pain, refusing to stop even after the creature's head was beaten to a pulp.

Primal

Kaito eased the piece of wood out of his wife's hands as she rose it over her head for the tenth time.

"Enough, Ichiko," he told her gently, letting the wood drop to the floor.

The primal rage finally eased out of her. She turned to her husband, staring into his eyes.

"It's dead, honey," Kaito told her, nodding to confirm it. "It's over."

Ichiko threw her arms around him. Kaito hugged her back, catching a whiff of her coconut shampoo even through the thick smell of blood. He kissed the top of her head a few times.

"What the hell is that thing…" Xavier asked, shining his flashlight on the creature but not daring to step any closer to it, even though its head was a still, bloody mess.

Ichiko had beaten the thing's head in so bad that its face was hardly recognizable as a face. Its teeth were pointing every which way and pieces of skull protruded out through the skin like shards of glass. Underneath this mess, a pool of its blood stretched away in snaky tendrils.

"An alien?" Kaito said, separating from Ichiko.

"An… alien?" Xavier echoed, more to himself than anyone.

He shined the flashlight over the creature's body, inspecting it more closely with this idea in mind.

While Xavier was doing that, Kaito walked over to Santiago's corpse. He wasn't sure when the man had passed away, but there was no doubt that he was dead. He crouched down in front of the dead man, who seemed oddly at peace despite the knife sticking out of his neck and all the blood covering his throat. Kaito closed his eyes and bowed out of respect. Then, he grabbed the knife and pulled it out of the corpse. Fresh blood gurgled up and spilled out of the wound as the blade slid out of the corpse.

Using the end of Santiago's sweater, Kaito wiped the blade clean of blood. It felt rude to do this, *but dead men don't complain,* Kaito thought to himself.

He held the blade up closer to the light to get a better look at it. The knife, much like the creature, was strangely familiar. It was a hunting knife, meant to puncture through an animal's hide, and it should've been heavy. But it wasn't. It was light.

Impossibly light.

"This must be from another planet, too," Kaito said, getting up and turning to Ichiko and Xavier. The knife was laying across his open hands, he held it out to them so they could get a better look at it.

Xavier didn't know what the man was talking about, but he didn't like it. "We need to get out of here." At this point, he no longer cared what was going on. Aliens or not, it was clear they were in danger.

"Yes, we must leave," Kaito said, putting the alien knife in one of his belt loops. "The only question is, which way to go?"

"Upstairs," Xavier said. "Norman is up there. He needs me."

"Your dog is not up there my friend," Kaito said, sternly.

"Y-you don't know that."

Kaito crossed the cellar, back to the boxes where he'd been rummaging before the alien dropped in, and started digging through them again. "If your dog is still there, Xavier, he is likely dead."

From one of the boxes he pulled out a staff t-shirt for the diner with a big St. Patrick's Day shamrock on the front with the words SAL'S DINER across the middle of it. Using the alien knife, he started cutting the shirt into strips.

"Going up there," Kaito continued, "is almost a guarantee we run into danger. We'll have a better chance out in the open."

Xavier didn't respond. Instead, he looked behind him at the staircase leading outside. The light coming in from the open doors let him see that a small mound of snow had formed at the top step. Beyond that, all he could see was the white of snowfall, obscuring the world around them.

No telling what was out there.

"In the diner, we'd at least have the walls to protect us," Xavier argued. Then he pointed outside. "We'll be blind out there. Defenseless."

"Someone stabbed Santiago," Kaito said. Walking over to Ichiko with the strips of fabric he started to bandage up her shoulder. "He tried to go upstairs and look at what happened to him."

"What if the aliens' ship is out there? Waiting for us with—I don't know—their guns already pointed at us? Upstairs we'd at least have windows to look out of." He tried to keep pushing for them all to go upstairs, but he knew Kaito had valid points. Norman might be alive, and he might not be, but either way there was someone up there who wanted them all to hurt.

And suffer.

Ichiko winced as Kaito began to tighten up the wraps.

"Hold still," Kaito told her. "Almost done. Done. Is that okay?"

"It's fine," Ichiko said, but her teeth were gritted together in pain.

Xavier walked over to one of the walls and leaned his back against it. He sighed, feeling defeated. They were right. They needed to get as far away from this diner as possible, even if that meant going out into the snow to do it.

"We will run to our cabin," Kaito said, giving him a reassuring nod. "It is not far from here. We can make it."

One last point of contention dawned on Xavier. "Why hasn't the person who killed Santiago come down to get us?"

"They might be waiting for us to go up there first." Kaito looked over at the dead creature laying on the ground. "I think maybe that thing was sent to get us going up there. To herd us."

"Like… a hunting dog?"

"Yes, Precisely." Kaito said, finishing up with Ichiko's bandages.

Xavier felt he was right. The thing had been quick and dangerous, but they'd overwhelmed it by working together. If it'd only been two of them, he wasn't so sure they would've been able to win. Also, the thing had stood down at the first sign of danger, as if it'd been holding back.

His hopes of seeing his dog were dwindling, and they couldn't stay in here longer. Xavier put his hands in his pockets and slumped his shoulders. "Fine. Let's go out the back then."

Kaito nodded.

"But one last thing," Xavier said, before they started to go, "I'm turning back at the first sign of danger."

"Sure." Kaito said.

"How far is the cabin?"

"Half a mile, maybe a little more."

"We can get there in less than thirty minutes if we hurry," Ichiko added.

"I have guns there," Kaito told Xavier. "We'll be safer there than here, where our only weapons are kitchenware."

Seeing the expression of concern still on Xavier's face, Kaito walked over to him and clapped him on the shoulder.

"I was in the Japanese army. This isn't my first time being in a dangerous situation. We will be okay, friend."

"That's good to know." Xavier said, casting one last glance up the stairs.

Norman couldn't be heard up there anymore. Kaito was right. His dog was either gone or dead. He had to give up on trying to save his dog—for now, at least—and instead, focus on staying alive.

Surgical

The closer they got to the top of the stairs, the slower they went. They'd made up their mind that this was the way they were going, but that didn't make it any easier.

Kaito put his foot on the top step, avoiding the trail of blood they'd seen earlier. The step creaked underneath his boot.

From here, he could see past the concrete sides of the entryway and had a better view of the lay of the land. He scanned their surroundings. The problem was, he could only see maybe five or six feet through white haze of the snowfall. There was no ship waiting for them with its guns drawn on them as Xavier had feared, that much he was sure of.

A gust blew, slinging snowflakes at his face like missiles, making him wish he'd grabbed his winter coat off the rack before heading out here.

Of course, that would have meant going back upstairs to get it, and that was out of the question.

Without realizing he'd done it, he'd taken several steps out from the doorway, and behind him he heard Ichiko and Xavier shuffling in the snow with him. He felt Ichiko's hand touch the small of his back as she came to his side.

"Look," she said, pointing at a deep furrow in the snow.

Kaito had missed it because he'd been more focused on what was in the distance. The trail was wide, and recent enough that the storm hadn't covered it up, and they could see the splashes of blood in it. The three of them immediately knew what it meant.

"It's Sal's blood," Xavier said, coming up next to the couple. "Right?"

Kaito nodded. "Yes. The alien must've gotten him while he was in the cellar and dragged him out here."

Their original plan had been to come out of the cellar doors and run as fast as they could toward the cabin, but this was throwing a wrench into that plan. Ichiko recognized the look of deep thought on her husband's face.

"You're thinking something," she told him. "Are you sensing danger?"

Kaito almost laughed. "I can barely feel my toes, Ichiko. I am not sure any of my senses are working properly in this cold."

"Then what is it?" she asked, more urgent this time.

Instead of answering her, he stepped forward. He was the one leading the way, so the others followed closely behind him. They walked alongside the bloody furrow, making a fresh trail of their own footprints in the snow.

"Yo, man, what is it?" Xavier said, getting worried.

But he didn't get an answer either. Kaito picked up the pace because now he was getting desperate for answers himself.

They walked a few more feet, and then the end of the trail emerged out of the stom, with Sal's body right there.

Or rather, what was left of it.

The diner owner was laying on his back, his arms sprawled out like a kid in mid-motion of making a snow angel. Part of his throat had been torn out and blood had pooled around the wound. His legs had been torn or bitten off his body just below the hips. There was no doubt in Kaito's mind that the alien creature from the cellar had done this.

But then, the damage done to his torso told a different story entirely.

The torso had been sliced down the middle, navel to breastbone, then pulled apart so that his skin laid over in two equally sized flaps on opposite sides of the body. All of his internal organs were simply gone, except for the intestines. They had been set aside, neatly coiled up like they were extra computer cables.

There was something precise about how it had been done.

"What the fuck..." Xavier whispered, feeling his stomach twisting over on itself at the sight. Something about the contrast of the two separate mutilations made it that much more disturbing.

"There are two aliens," Kaito said. He was sure of it now. The attack on Santiago had been different than the attack by the creature. It had seemed to him like the work of two different beings before. Now this confirmed it. "The one we killed in the cellar must be some sort of hunting creature—an alien dog, something like that. And then, the one that killed Santiago and performed this...um, surgery on Sal, must be more humanoid."

"Whatever the deal is, it's clear we need to get out of here," Xavier said, starting through the snow.

Even so, Kaito stayed where he was. A morbidly curious part of his mind was fascinated with the idea of an alien performing surgery to harvest organs from a human, and he wanted just a few more minutes to examine it. But there was no time for that. The longer they were out here, the more danger they were in.

"Kaito, we have to go," Ichiko said to him, grabbing his arm.

She went up on her tiptoes and planted a kiss on his cheek. The snowflakes that had been clinging to their skin melted between the contact.

"Let's go home," Ichiko said, pulling him after Xavier.

Aim

Crouched over a black case, the Visitor was using a pair of small tongs to pick up and inspect the organs he'd extracted from the human his dog had dragged out of the shelter. He'd let the dog chew and tear anything on the body to reward him. Everything except the organs, that is, because those were meant to be brought back to the ship.

The Visitor gave the liver squeezed between his tongs one last look-over. He wouldn't be able to determine where to taxonomically classify this species without running it under the proper machinery, but there was something fascinating about the insides of primitive species.

Done with looking it over, he stuffed the liver back into the case, right between one of the kidneys and the heart, slipped the tongs into a pocket on the inside of the lid, and closed the case. He left it in the snow as he surveyed his surroundings.

From the rooftop of the diner, he had a three-sixty view of his surroundings. The dog should have returned from his task of scaring the Earthlings out of the shelter. Enough time had lapsed for that... Which meant something was wrong...

In the distance, the Visitor saw the three Earthlings running through the snow.

He waited a few beats to see if the hunting dog was running after them. It wasn't, which meant the humans must've maimed or slain it.

The Visitor was unconcerned with this, as they had more hunting dogs back home. What he needed to focus on was getting more organs.

The Visitor unslung the rifle around his shoulders, then laid down flat on the snowy roof. From studying the Earthling lying in the snow, he knew where their weaknesses were. All he had to do was aim and shoot.

They ran through the snow as fast as they could, but it was like the elements were uniting to make it as difficult as possible. Wind pushed against them, blowing huge snowflakes into their faces, hindering their sight. The cold was beginning to harden the snow, making it harder to take each step.

But they kept pushing, kept pumping their legs as fast as they could, knowing that with each step they put Sal's Diner farther and farther behind them. And at the same time—hopefully—that meant leaving the danger behind, too.

Laser

Since they knew the way, Kaito and Ichiko took the lead again. That was how Xavier saw the three red dots appear on the back of Kaito's thigh. Before Xavier could even form the words to warn him, the three red dots blinked out. Then, a blast of bright light shot through the air, so fast and sudden it burned a line across Xavier's sight.

The blast burned through the air, melting snow to splashes of water as it traveled toward its target. The laser tore through the back of Kaito's leg, blowing a chunk out of it. He fell to his knees in the snow, screaming in pain, dropping his flashlight. He pressed his hand against the gaping hole in his leg as blood seeped through his fingers.

The red lights appeared on Kaito's body again, this time on his back. They began to move upward, crawling like a bug searching for the perfect spot to bite down on, up to his neck, and then settled on his head...

Oh shit, Xavier thought.

A headshot. The person behind the weapon was looking for a headshot to finish him off.

Xavier and Ichiko had stopped running when they saw the flash and heard Kaito scream. Ichiko had screamed in fear, but now rushed to get to her husband's side.

But Kaito had no chance. With only one leg and the lasers already on him, Xavier knew the only thing she would accomplish was getting herself killed.

Instincts took over, and he lunged at her with his arms open. He grabbed her by the waist and pulled her away. Ichiko kicked her legs out, but Xavier overpowered her. He picked her up and started running the opposite way.

He scanned ahead of them and could just see a patch of trees in the distance. They were dead and bare this time of the year, but some cover would be better than no cover. He thought he'd been running as fast as he could before, but now that they were in grave danger again, he kicked it into another gear.

Behind them, the laser found its target. Pure heat shot through the air and passed through Kaito's head, obliterating the top of his skull. Cooked matter oozed out of the hole, melting the snow it touched into steam.

Xavier made it to the trees, and dove behind a large oak, still clutching Ichiko in his arms. At this point, she'd given up trying to fight him, so she went with him as he sat down with his back pressed against the tree trunk.

Ichiko wrapped her arms around Xavier's neck and buried her face into his chest and cried. She cried harder than Xavier had ever heard anyone cry before in his life. He wasn't sure if it was the quietness of the snowstorm making it sound louder, but it was heart-wrenching to hear.

He held her tighter, and then something compelled him to kiss the top of her head. It wasn't a romantic kiss in the slightest, more like what one family member gives to another when mourning the loss of a loved one. They'd only met a few short hours ago, but the experience of fighting for survival had formed a bridge between them neither had realized until now.

Until there were only two of them left.

Out the corner of his eye, Xavier saw three red dots sweep across the trees. The lights were coming from behind them, which thankfully meant the tree they were leaning against blocked them from view.

The red lights moved up and down and across the trees, reflecting off the snow and refracting the flakes dropping out of the sky, like a predator looking for its prey, until it concentrated on a branch several trees from where they were.

In the blink of an eye another burning laser bolt pierced the air and cut through the branch. It fell off the tree, charred where the laser had gone through it, and fell silently into the snow.

"They're trying to scare us into coming out of hiding," Xavier whispered to Ichiko as he realized what was going on. She snuffled, took a second to compose herself, and then nodded in agreement.

The red dots appeared again, moving along the trees. They settled on another branch, this one bigger and closer to them, but still just as random of a target as the first. Then a laser bolt tore it from the tree and sent it crashing through smaller branches to send up a plume of snow from the ground. It was startling, but there was nothing threatening about it. Whoever was trying to kill them was shooting blind.

The red lights moved around randomly for several more seconds, and then made a quick motion to the left before disappearing entirely.

"They can't find us," Ichiko guessed.

"Seems that way," Xavier said, resting his head against the trunk of the tree and closing his eyes.

He had no idea when it would be safe to move again, but he did know one thing. They would have to wait here, for now.

Despite the cold and the storm, he was ready to wait a very long time if it meant surviving.

Tracks

The Visitor walked through the snow, following the tracks his targets left behind. He walked past the Earthling he'd just shot. Unfortunately, his brain was half-cooked and would be useless, but he would still come back to the body to extract the other organs. First, he had to make sure the other two didn't get away.

Once at the tree line, the Visitor stopped. He carried the case with the organs to the nearest tree and hung it on one the lower branches by the handle. The material it was made out of was weatherproof and could sustain most planets' atmospheres, but it was better this way. It would save him the trouble of having to find it buried in the snow later.

The Visitor unstrapped his rifle, readied it, and inspected the area. The disturbed path through the snow continued a few feet ahead and then bent around a tree with a broad trunk. He looked ahead, and didn't see any sign of the trail continuing, suggesting this was where the targets must be hiding.

Simple prey equaled a simple hunt.

The Visitor took aim with his rifle.

Xavier and Ichiko were both poking their heads around the tree, just enough for them to see the alien a few feet away. He wore a black body suit that was skintight against his slender frame, with a small air tank hanging from the back that was connected to the back of the helmet by a gray hose.

The front of the helmet was see-through glass, and with the backlights around the visor they could see the alien's massive eyes moving as he traced their path through the snow. He got to the end of the trail, then looked up at the oak tree. The pale gray face had no expression, but Xavier and Ichiko both knew he'd figured out where they were. The snow had given them away.

They watched the alien raise a weapon that looked something like a rifle and take aim right at the oak. He was going to shoot through it, to get to them.

It was time to run.

There was no plan. They were relying purely on instinct. They ran in opposite directions. Ichiko to the right, Xavier to the left.

Xavier passed in front of the alien, making him the easier of the two targets.

The Visitor pivoted on his heels, rifle aimed, in Xavier's direction. The red dots found their target…and then Xavier cut diagonally to the left. The sudden change threw the Visitor off and bought Xavier time to disappear behind another tree.

The Visitor fired.

The blast from the gun pierced through the tree and blurred right past Xavier, missing him by mere inches. He'd slowed his pace down, anticipating the shot, hoping the unseen change in pace would throw the aliens' aim off. The trick had worked.

The blast continued, going right through two more trees before dissipating. Then Xavier picked up his pace.

The Visitor saw him emerge from behind the tree, running fast and kicking up snow with every step. He swept the rifle to put Xavier back into his sight, but Xavier zagged, and then dodged again. He was using all of the athleticism and skills he'd gained from playing football in school, and the Visitor couldn't keep up with it.

Xavier disappeared behind another tree, going as fast as he could, hoping the change in timing would throw the alien off.

But this time, there was no shot.

As he sprinted past the tree, Xavier looked over his shoulder and saw why.

The alien's attention had gone elsewhere.

Lost

Norman raced through the trees, and as he closed in on the alien, he hopped up and bit him in the crotch.

The Visitor stepped back, taking one hand off his rifle and reaching into the utility belt at his waist. He pulled out a long knife as the dog growled and kept its bite on him, trying to pull him off his feet.

Norman saw the blade, and no matter how much he wanted to save his human he knew he was in danger. He let go and started to run as the Visitor slashed the knife at him.

The blade cut the dog in the back of the neck. Norman yelped and started limping backward as fast as he could. He slipped in the snow, recovered, then changed direction and darted out of the trees, disappearing into the white void of the snow once again.

The Visitor fell to one knee, holding onto the painful area of the bite, trying to recover from the attack. He wasn't making any noise, as his kind didn't feel pain like other beings did.

While the alien had been fighting off the Border Collie, Ichiko had managed to circle around him. She was charging him from behind now, knife clutched tight in her hands. With a scream that shattered the snow-heavy silence she jumped onto the alien's back and drove the knife deep through the suit. She'd meant to get it in the neck, but she missed by mere inches and hit somewhere above the collarbone.

The Visitor reached behind with both hands for her. Ichiko saw, and pulled the knife out to stab it through the palms of one of the gloves. She found her target and the knife skewered out the other side of that hand. She let out a cry that was both victorious and enraged.

But the battle wasn't over, the alien's other hand grabbed a fistful of her hair. With a quick whip of his body and a hard tug the Visitor threw Ichiko off his back. She hit the ground and sank into the soft piles of snow. Flailing her arms, kicking her legs, she managed to get back up onto her feet and started running through the trees. With the sneak attacking having failed, she didn't like her chances.

Reaching down for another one of his hunting knives, the Visitor pursued her.

Even through the snowfall, Xavier knew the blur that had raced through the trees had been Norman. Hope surged when he saw his pup, alive, and he knew he had to turn back. The dog had been brave enough to try to save them all. He needed to do what he could for Ichiko now.

He raced through the snow, trying to close the gap between him and the alien, who was now chasing Ichiko through the trees.

Xavier had no idea what he was going to do once he got there, but he knew he had to try something. He ran, and he slipped, and he almost fell, and then right in front of him he saw something, dark and long sticking out of the snow.

As he got closer he realized what it was. The alien's weapon. The barrel of the rifle was buried a few inches in the snow, butt up in the air.

Xavier picked it up, and despite how smooth it was it fit well in his hands, and it was easy to hold. Whatever it was made of seemed to change properties where his hands touched it, turning almost sticky.

If he'd doubted Kaito's conclusion before, he didn't now. He was holding alien technology in his hands.

Later, he would dwell on the amazement of this. Right now, he had to put it to use.

Xavier looked up from the weapon.

The alien was chasing Ichiko through the trees, and his back was to Xavier. He moved with cumbersome strides, obviously injured from the knife wounds Ichiko gave him and the bite from Norman, but the alien's legs were long and spindly, and he would catch up to her in no time.

Xavier ran toward them, trying to angle himself for a better shot at the alien. It was going to be risky. The laser blasts had passed right through thick trees like they weren't even there. If he shot through the alien, he'd kill Ichiko, too. If he ran more to his left, he could get the right angle, and kill this fucker while saving their lives.

He hoped.

Dismemberment

chiko slipped on frozen snow and dropped into a thicket of bushes. As she tumbled deeper into them, some of the sharp ends of the branches tore into her clothes and skin. Ichiko flipped over her own head once before she lost her momentum, landing flat on her back.

From the corners of her vision she saw the alien coming toward her. He was upside down to her, and she was a bit dizzy, but she could tell he was gaining on her.

She had to move.

Ichiko tried untangling herself from the bushes but something tugged at her pantleg, keeping her in place. She looked down and saw a long branch had not just torn through her jeans but was completely wrapped around her in a tangle.

"*Kuso,*" Ichiko hissed. She bent down and tugged at the plant's grip, hoping either the fabric would tear, or the branch would break.

Neither one of those things happened.

The alien was seconds away.

Ichiko wrenched on her jeans, this time kicking her leg to add some force. There was a loud rip as the denim tore, but it wasn't enough. The alien's dark form paused above her. The hand wielding the knife raised up over its head, getting ready to bring it plunging down. The gray face inside the helmet was expressionless, not so much as a hint of strain or pain as he prepared to kill her.

Before he could bring the knife down, three red dots popped into being on the alien's shoulder. A second later, the dots blinked out and a brilliant light streaked through the air. The blast from the rifle tore through the alien's arm, sending it spinning out into the snow. Mid-arc, the fingers on the hand uncurled, and the knife went tumbling through the air.

Blood sprayed out from the wound, dark but not quite red, and even then, the alien's expression didn't change. He simply looked down at his missing appendage, and then turned in the direction where the laser blast had come from.

Ichiko saw the knife land in the snow, blade down and handle up, just past where the bushes held her captive. She stretched as the alien's attention was distracted. Her fingertips touched the cold handle, but she couldn't quite get it yet.

With a big grunt, she forced herself forward and managed another inch. Her hands closed around the blade, and she brought the knife around and cut her pantleg off the bush. Ichiko got to her feet, scrambled away, and saw Xavier standing behind a tree nearby. He had the alien's weapon in his hands and was aiming it at the alien.

The Visitor stared back at the Earthling, a blank expression on his face despite the blood pouring out of the wound where his arm had been shot off. Xavier lined the barrel up with the alien's chest, took in a deep breath, and pulled on the trigger.

But the trigger wouldn't budge.

Xavier tried again, but it didn't work. It wouldn't budge. Like the thing was frozen. He looked back up at the alien. It had it's one remaining arm extended, the fingertips glowing orange.

The barrel of the rifle detached from the gun, and then the other parts began to fall apart in equally sized blocks. The blocks that had once made up the gun floated in the air for a few seconds, then dropped to the ground leaving Xavier with nothing.

Knife in hand, Ichiko lunged at the alien. She slashed at him, but he saw it coming and simply stepped out of the way. She missed, and the alien grabbed her by the wrist as her own motion carried her past. The Visitor tossed her to the ground but kept ahold of her wrist. He wrenched her arm the wrong way, and Ichiko screamed. The knife slipped out of her hand. She felt something crunch in her arm, and pain radiated down the length of her spine.

The Visitor let go of her and bent down to pick up the knife. Xavier saw what was coming and felt powerless to stop it. He had nothing. No weapon. All he had was the pieces...

Inspiration flashed through his mind and he bent down to pick up one of the metal cubes. He chucked it at the alien as hard as he could. It hit the side of his helmet hard enough to make the alien stumble. Then, out of desperation and because he had nothing left but himself, Xavier charged at him, shoulder lowered, and rammed the alien as hard as he could.

The knife went flying out of the Visitor's hand as Xavier drove them into a tree. They bounced off and went sprawling into the snow.

Xavier laid in the snow, his ears ringing, his vision blurry.

Meanwhile, the Visitor got up to his feet like it was nothing. He turned to where the metal cubes were and extended his arm out, his fingertips glowing again as he activated the technology in the gloves. The metal blocks levitated into the air, and then they came together, snapping into place like a jigsaw puzzle building itself. Once the rifle was back together, it turned and floated back into the alien's hand.

Before he could aim, Ichiko jumped onto his back. She wrapped her legs around his waist to secure herself, then slashed with the knife she had picked up again. Only this time, her target wasn't the alien himself.

It was the air tank on the alien's back.

There was a loud pop as the blade cut through the vinyl hose, followed by a hiss as whatever gas was in there came rushing out.

The Visitor thrashed his body and began to convulse. He dropped the rifle to reach back and push Ichiko off but she was already hopping off him. The alien's glove came up to his throat, grabbing there like he was choking.

Which was exactly what was happening.

Dark green veins bulged in the alien's gray face as Earth's air entered its helmet through the cut hose. Something in the atmosphere was poisoning it. There was finally an expression there, but it was impossible to read. Pain? Fear? There was no way to know.

The Visitor dropped down to his knees, his entire body shaking like it was about to explode. He fell over onto his back, his legs twitching and kicking wildly. His single arm flailed through the air as the cold air of earth filled his lungs.

Ichiko found the rifle in the snow, picked it up, and stood over the alien with it. She put a boot on his chest to pin him down and put the barrel of the rifle up to the helmet and pulled the trigger.

The glass on the helmet evaporated, and the alien's head exploded as the laser passed through it. Save for a few twitches here and there, the Visitor's body went still.

Ichiko fell back onto her haunches into the snow. The rifle dropped out of her hands, but she was happy to let it go. She had avenged her husband's death, and she had saved their lives. It was enough.

Now that it was over, or at least seemed to be over, the reality of everything hit her. Tears began rolling down her cheeks, and her chest tightened around her heart.

She went to scrub at the tears falling out of her eyes, but felt a hand stop her. It was Xavier, standing over her. His hair was thrown every which way on his head, and he was covered in snow, but there was a weak smile on his face.

Still holding onto her hand, he sat down next to her. Gently, he used his own sleeve to wipe her tears away. He put his arm around her shoulders and squeezed her close to him.

For a few minutes, they sat like that, watching the alien's twitching lessening by the second.

"It's over," Xavier announced. He wasn't sure if he was saying that to Ichiko or to himself, but either way, it felt appropriate.

Ichiko put her head against his shoulder, and let the tears fall as they would.

Crackling

A crackling sound coming from somewhere on the alien's spacesuit brought Ichiko out of her sobbing. She lifted her head off Xavier's shoulder, and wiping the snot off her nose with the sleeve of her jacket, looked over at the corpse.

The crackling turned into static, and then a voice came through a speaker built into the alien's helmet. "*Krokatart... T'rakok...Krokatart...? T'rakok?*"

Ichiko recognized some of that as the same message that had been going through the landline back in the diner. Only this seemed to be a different voice.

Xavier got up to his feet and took a few steps closer to the Visitor. The crackling had stopped for now, but he could hear a small hissing as the last of the supply inside the air tank came out of the cut hose. He bent down closer, to where he could see lights flashing on the utility belt.

Ichiko stood and turned her back. "I don't want to look at it," Ichiko said.

Before Xavier could say anything, another message came through the speaker.

"*Krokatart...? Orkitarar... U'kerk...*" This time the tone was urgent.

Hearing the alien language sent a chill down Xavier's spine.

"We have to get out of here," he said.

Ichiko nodded. She agreed, although she didn't know why. Something was wrong. She could feel it in her bones.

"They're...coming for him," Xavier said, looking up at the sky, expecting to see a spacecraft flying through the air. "That message. I think they're asking him if he needs to be rescued."

"If that is true, it is best we're not here when they arrive," Ichiko said.

Without another word, they started their way back to the cabin.

The snow had let up in the last five minutes since they'd been walking, making visibility better. About a quarter of a mile ahead of them, the Takahashis cabin came into view, lit up from the lights they'd left on before going out for their hike earlier in the day.

The cabin's rooftop and awning were covered with over a foot of snow. It was a tiny, humble little thing that had just the bare minimum in it to be considered a shelter, but Xavier had never felt more relieved to see a place in his life.

"Look!" Ichiko said, stopping and pointing up at the sky.

Xavier stopped at the sound of her voice. He looked up at the sky and saw something shiny floating in the distance.

It moved left and right, but not like an airplane at all. It seemed to be moving as if on an invisible track in the sky, changing directions without losing or having to build any sort of momentum. Moving in a way that defied the laws of physics of Earth.

Then, the object started flying toward them. Almost in the blink of an eye, the thing went from being distant and tiny to huge and right over their heads. The ship gleamed with internal light.

Ichiko and Xavier turned around to trace its flight as it continued flying by at an unbelievable speed, until it stopped a good distance behind them, where they'd left the dead alien. The object stayed still, hanging in the sky. It was there long enough for them to see that it was disc-shaped, with no gaps or breaks in it, so that it just one enormous and solid object.

The spacecraft dipped down suddenly, moving in that seemingly impossible way again. The bottom half of the ship was lost behind the hill to Ichiko and Xavier, so they couldn't see what was going on. But they could guess.

This spacecraft was here to take the Visitor away—or rather, take his corpse away, back to wherever their home planet was.

Without needing to build up any momentum, the ship lifted up into sight again, and flew skyward, shooting through the air like a silver bullet. Each second it shrank smaller and smaller, until it was nothing more than a twinkle against the dark sky.

A second later, it winked out of sight entirely.

Cabin

They were sitting on the porch, in a wooden loveseat that took up most of the space, sipping on Earl Grey tea from tin cups. The snowfall was dying off, reduced to nothing more than some light flurries. The wind had lost its vigor, too, and the night surrounded them.

Xavier set the tin cup on the armrest, next to the pistol Ichiko had given him from Kaito's gun stash. He got up, stuffing the gun inside his jacket.

"You're leaving?" Ichiko asked.

"Yeah," Xavier said, zipping his jacket up. "I'm going to go find my dog."

"You think he's still out there?"

Xavier shrugged. "I won't know for sure unless I go looking for him, right?"

"I suppose." Ichiko said, then paused to drink some of her tea. She brought the cup up to her mouth with both hands. "Are you going back there? Back to the diner, I mean?"

"Yeah. Even if I don't find Norm, at least when I get back there, I can see if any of our cellphones are working and call for help."

Ichiko picked her cell phone off the armrest and unlocked it. There was no service. Of course not. Her and Kaito had never had cell phone service out in this cabin. The disconnect had been a part of the appeal for them. In the current situation, though, not so much.

Xavier put his hood up and started down the porch steps. Halfway down, he stopped and turned to Ichiko.

"Hey… Uh, I'm real sorry about your husband." There was a sudden lump in his throat, and he had to swallow it back.

"Me too." Ichiko said, her eyes dropping down to her tea.

"Are you…going to be okay? Here by yourself, I mean." Xavier paused. "You can come with me, if you want."

Ichiko shook her head. "I will be okay. Eventually."

"We were so damn close." Xavier said, kicking some snow off the steps. "The others, maybe we couldn't have done anything for them, but Kaito. He almost made it, if only we would've stopped and looked around or ran for the trees faster—"

"You should go," Ichiko said, picking up her teacup and taking a quick sip of it. "Before it gets darker."

"Yeah," Xavier said, feeling defeated. He put his hands in his pockets and sighed. "Thanks for everything. Take care."

"You too, my friend."

Friend. The word echoed through his head—redefined, now—as he waved to her, turned around and started the trek back to the diner.

Return

The Christmas lights Sal had hung around the diner came into view, the only color to an otherwise drab landscape. Xavier stopped at the top of the hill before going any further. Norm hadn't been anywhere, and he didn't see him anywhere now.

Surveying the area below him he saw some red spots here and there in the snow revealed by the flashlight. He knew there were dead bodies out there, and he didn't want to see any of them.

Xavier started down the hill, heading toward the parking lot. He decided to start from there and work his way into the diner. He wasn't sure who he was going to call to tell them aliens had killed all these people, but there had to be someone.

As he came to the parking lot, he heard music coming from a Honda Fit. That must've been Moshe's car. The engine was still on, so some of the snow had melted off the hood. From inside, he heard a radio jockey wish everyone happy holidays before a commercial for some department store's after Christmas sale came on.

Xavier walked around to the driver side and saw the remains of the comedian-poet he'd met a few hours ago. The alien dog must've gotten to him because his body was chewed up. Chunks of flesh had been bitten off all the limbs, and his head was missing.

For the first time that night, Xavier turned away and nearly threw up. His stomach surged, but he managed to keep ahold of himself.

He turned away to look at the highway. His wrecked car was likely out there in the same spot, but it wasn't going to do him anymore good now than it did when this whole nightmare started.

Xavier stood there, watching the road for a few minutes, noticing that not a single car passed by. Of course not. It was still Christmas. Everyone was cozied up at home with their families. It wasn't even late enough for the novelty of their presents to have worn off yet.

They'd probably been watching the snowfall with glee, glad to have gotten a white Christmas this year.

Better than a red one, Xavier thought, as he turned to head into the diner.

The bells on the holly jingled as he came through the door, just like the first time he and Santiago had come into Sal's Diner. Except this time, he was solo, and instead of holiday music filling the air, it was the stench of death.

The place was silent. In the corner, the sparsely decorated Christmas tree and untouched presents looked sad.

Xavier walked through the diner and sat down underneath the Christmas lights; in the same spot he'd been in earlier in the night. In front of him, the mug he'd been drinking out of still had about a quarter of coffee left in it. He picked it up and drank it in one swig, despite it being cold and bitter. He didn't care. It felt right. Like the action was a form of paying respects to those that had died today.

Xavier turned in the stool and looked across the diner. Norm's blue leash was still tied to the table, but it'd been cut. The alien had shown his dog mercy, for some reason. Maybe because he had a hunting dog of his own, or maybe it'd just been here on a mission to collect human organs and there hadn't been a reason for him to kill the Border Collie.

Thinking of his dog made him sad, but he tried to ignore the feeling as he shifted his focus to his jacket, which was still hanging on the back of the stool. He reached into it for his cell phone, clicked the side button to unlock the screen, and saw there were two bars of service.

It was either a Christmas miracle, or the alien had been jamming electronic devices somehow. He thought of the flashing light he'd seen on his utility belt, and figured the latter was likely the answer. Either way, it didn't really matter. The important thing was he could call for help now.

But how the hell am I supposed to explain all this? Xavier thought, looking over at the cellar door. It was ajar and let him see some of the darkness of the staircase.

He was going through the different ways to try to explain it to the police in his head, when he heard something climbing up the cellar stairs. There was a click of paws against wood, then it stopped, and a pair of eyes stared at him through the crack in the door.

Xavier rose out of the stool and reached into his pocket for the gun. Before he could point it, the door was pushed open as the animal behind it came barreling out.

Panting, covered in blood, with his tongue out, Norman pranced into the diner.

"Norm!" Xavier hollered, putting the gun on the counter, and racing over to meet his dog.

The dog jumped up, licking at Xavier's hands, wagging his tail, and barking excitedly. Xavier gave him a big hug. The dog was soaking wet and smelled funky, but Xavier didn't care. He hugged him tight, only letting him go to look him over.

The fur on the top of his head was crusty from the blood where the alien had cut him with the knife, but it didn't appear to be anything more than a flesh wound. Xavier hugged him tight again and kissed him and told him he was a good boy. Norman woofed his flattery.

It turned out there'd been one more survivor of the Visitor, after all.

A loud, but muffled ringing broke the joyous moment.

Xavier let Norman go and turned his attention to the stools, where the sound was coming from. A phone was vibrating inside a gray windbreaker that had belonged to Santiago.

Xavier went over to it and searched the pockets and until he found the iPhone and pulled it out. In the center of the screen a message read: INCOMING FACETIME REQUEST FROM MI AMOR SILVIA.

It was Santiago's wife. Xavier couldn't remember if the man had told him his wife's name or not, but there was no doubt in his mind that's who this was.

Xavier sat back down on the stool. Norman licked at the melting snow stuck to the side of his boot. Typically, Xavier would have scolded him for doing something like this, but at the moment, his mind was elsewhere. He knew if he answered the FaceTime request, he would have to tell Santiago's wife the fate of her husband.

And if he didn't, she would likely be worried sick all night when she didn't hear back from him.

A lump formed in Xavier's throat as he found himself in a situation with no right decision.

"Looks like we're in a jam again, buddy," Xavier said to Norman, looking up from the phone to him, as if the dog would have the answer written on his face.

The dog stopped licking at Xavier's boots and gazed up at him, cocking his head to the side. The dog wasn't sure what was going on, but he sensed some distress from his human, so he let out a short yap of encouragement. Then he returned to licking water off the boots.

Xavier looked back down at the screen, where his own face was staring back at him and the FaceTime request was still incoming. He had to make a decision, or else the phone would do it for him. Xavier hovered his thumb over the DECLINE and ANSWER buttons for a second, before finally pressing his finger to the screen.

Afterword

The dog lived. Think of it as my gift to you.
Happy Holidays!
Thanks for reading,
S. Gomez 9/16/2020

Acknowledgments

First and foremost, I have to thank my friend Derrick. He's been supporting me nonstop since day one. Whether its listening to me ramble over the phone or giving me helpful feedback on these drafts, he's always finding a way to carve out time to be there for me. Without him, I don't know how I'd keep my head straight.

A big thank you to all of the people from social media who always seem to show support: Tav, Courtney, Sadie, Karlee, Alex, Danny, Ashley, Dez, V, Jordaline, RJ, and all of the rest of you who send me wonderful messages and post awesome pictures of my books.

About the Author

Born in Mexico but raised in the United States, Sergio Gomez lives in Philadelphia with his family. He enjoys reading, martial arts, cooking, but most of all writing. His favorite superhero is either Batman or Hellboy depending on the day. Sergio has written two other novels and a short-story collection.

You can follow him on social media:

Instagram: @sergiopgomez

Facebook.com/AuthorSergioGomez

Made in the USA
Las Vegas, NV
13 October 2023

79017424R00056